THE
GRITTERMAN

THE
GRITTERMAN

Orlando Weeks

PARTICULAR
BOOKS

PARTICULAR BOOKS

UK | USA | Canada | Ireland | Australia
India | New Zealand | South Africa

Particular Books is part of the Penguin Random House group of companies
whose addresses can be found at global.penguinrandomhouse.com.

Penguin
Random House
UK

First published by Particular Books 2017
Published in Penguin Books 2018
002

Text and Illustrations copyright © Orlando Weeks, 2017

The moral right of the author has been asserted

Printed and bound in Italy by L.E.G.O. S.p.A

A CIP catalogue record for this book is available from the British Library

ISBN: 978-0-141-98662-3

For KF

Listen to or download *The Gritterman*'s companion album
featuring 10 new tracks by Orlando Weeks.
Available now on all digital and streaming platforms.

In the summer my van is an ice-cream van and I am an ice-cream man.
Not that there's much of a summer round here.

If it's not dewy, it's drizzly. If it's not drizzly, it's spitting.
If it's not spitting, it's chucking it down or bucketing it down or
coming down in sheets.

Still, now and then the sun comes out for long enough to burn a
few bald heads and sell a few ice creams.

I've no real passion for ice cream, but it keeps
me busy while I wait for winter…

… when the van becomes a Gritting Van and I become a Gritterman.
Soon as the Christmas lights go up in the high street
I stock up on grit.

I've got two fibreglass 99s on the roof of the van. There's a feller in town that makes them. He reckons he can do any food in fibreglass. Whatever you want. They're temperamental things and one's melted a bit from a hot bulb.

Mister Softee

When they're not on the blink they light up and rotate, and as they turn they chime. Everything from 'Mr Mozart's Drawing Room' to 'Mr Softee's Jingle'. I have 'em on whether I'm selling ice or gritting it.

They'll ring out for the last time tonight.

Got sent a letter from the council. 'Dear Sir ...
Your services are no longer required.'

I've done more years gritting than there were letters in that letter.
But that's OK, I'm not much of a reader ...

'Gritting's a dying profession,' they tell me.
'The planet's heating up,' they say.

Truth of the matter, it's always the same. You dress for the sun and down comes the rain so you dress for the rain and the sun's out again. It's as old as the weather.

I read somewhere that there's a tarmac now that can de-ice itself. I'm not sure I want to live in a world where the B2116 doesn't need gritting.

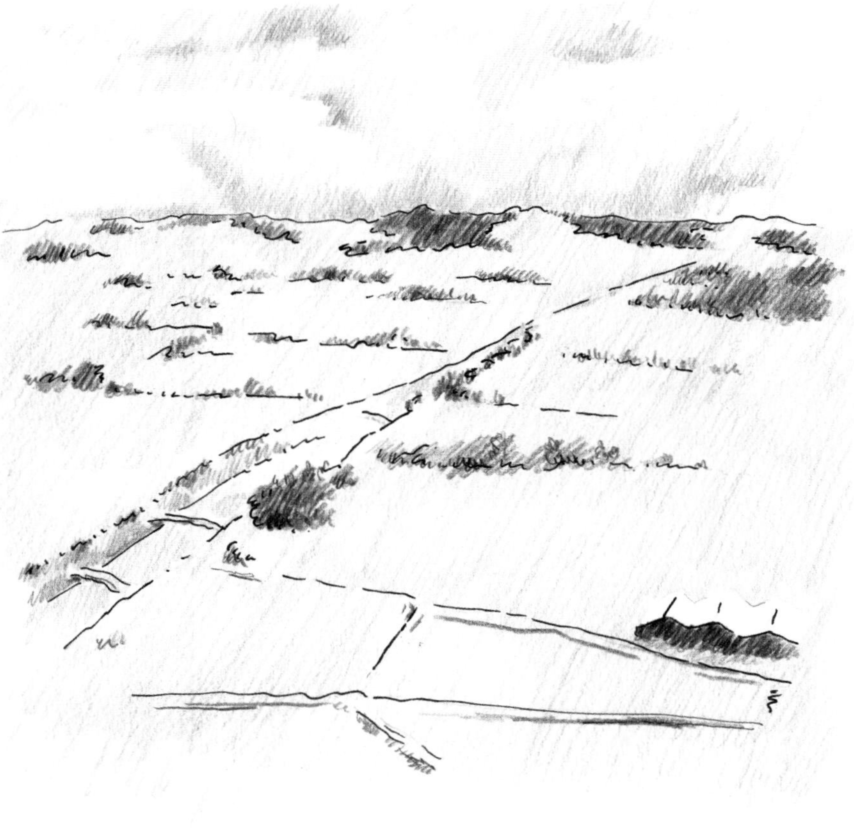

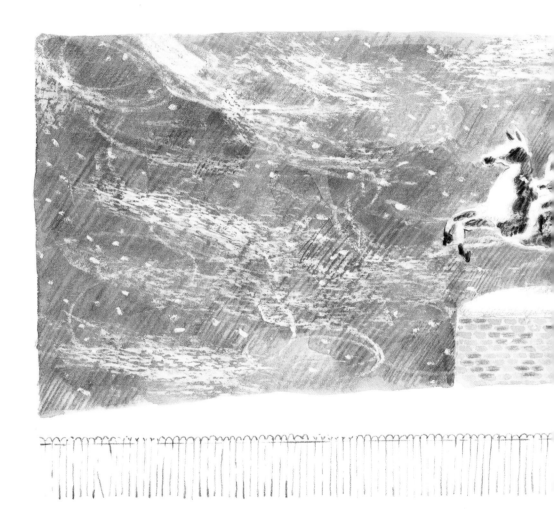

As a rule I do the local pavements and the footpaths before it gets dark.

Can't start on the roads too early. Too much traffic about.

But sometimes needs must.

When I've been out during the day I feel like some kind of seasonal hero.

On the narrower roads cars'll queue for hours behind me, just waiting their turn. Then one by one they drive past, cheering from their windows. Beeping their horns and flashing their lights.

Keeps me going it does.

This is my place, number 25. I've been here a good while. Not as long as the wallpaper but longer than the curtains.

I live alone these days. My Joy's sadly no longer with us.

The vicar tells me she's gritting my path to heaven. I told him that was unlikely. I think she might leave that job for me. She was good like that was my Joy, generous. Don't get me wrong, she had a temper. Cor! She could boil water with a look.

'I will miss her for her funny ways.
I will miss her for her turn of phrase.
I will miss her company on the slower days.
I will miss our singalongs to *Songs of Praise*.
I will not miss her soap-opera gossip about what he says
and she says and they says about what she says.
But in all other ways I will miss her.'

I read that at the service.

Six o'clock, radio should be on . . . mustn't miss the weather.
Last trip or not, I'll keep to time.

Huh . . . isn't that typical. Christmas Eve and the heavens open.
It's falling thick as vicar's dandruff out there. All sideways and angry.

Just look at that sky, like a dirty puddle, like the world's
been left alone.

Let it howl. Let it blow itself out. 'Snow before seven, fine by eleven.'
We'll have a moon tonight.

It's a wonderful thing, a moon. Whether it's as distant as a star or big enough to fill the windscreen, a cold blue slither or a fat burnt-orange disc, I don't mind.

I'd take the moon over the sun any day.

Hmmm, dinnertime I think . . .

Right, let's see what we have here then . . . Where are my specs? . . .
'Remove outer packaging . . . pierce film lid . . . place in microwave for
three minutes.' Three minutes, eh? Talk about the miracle of Christmas.

'Hummm humhum midwinter
Frosty wind made moan,
hummm humhum as iron,
Water like a stone;
Snow had fallen, snow on snow,
Snow on snow,
In the bleak midwinter
Long ago.'

I love that one. You never think of someone having to write Christmas carols. They're just sort of there, aren't they, like the *A to Z*.

There's the ping, that's dinner ready!

Turkey chow mein . . . delicious!

It's still at it out there. Funny stuff, snow. While it's falling it's constantly changing shape. It keeps changing, over and over and over. Right up until the moment it settles somewhere. Every shape and size and never the same twice. Floating earthward from that great height towards what it thinks might be 'its' place: some predetermined spot on a bus shelter or the head of a statue, or the hour hand of the town clock.

Until whoosh . . . it's blustered away and lands on a trawler destined for somewhere more exotic, like Gothenburg. Lost and confused things, snowflakes . . .

Oh, I must've dropped off.

Look at that, eleven o'clock. Time to get ready.

I've all your usual stuff. Thermals, jumper, scarf. The cap was my dad's. I don't bother with gloves any more. I only lose them. If you find a lonely glove on a railing, more likely than not it's one of mine.

These are my easy-to-put-on-nightmare-to-take-off double-thick waterproof waders. This right one is fantastic. This other one, however, has a hole in the heel. I've patched it with countless puncture repair kits, but I still get a soggy foot every night. I know what you're thinking: time for a new pair. But I can't just splash out on wellies.

Right . . . Am I ready?

Light's off. Heater's off. Cooker's off. Telly's off. Locked shed.
Cat's fed. Well what the cat actually is *rhymes* with fed . . . Anyhow.

Locked shed. Cat's fed. Hot water bottle's in bed. Thermos of soup.
Thermos of tea. What am I forgetting? . . . The van key.
That was Joy's line.

Off we go.

Here she is. Talk about last legs. I wouldn't buy her,
but I wouldn't sell her either.

She's a single-seater in questionable condition with mossy
window sealants, rusty skirting and a dink on the left wheel arch
that's the same shape as Scotland.

On the plus side, when the windscreen wipers are going full pelt they make a beautiful 'waffopping' sound. Like geese wings on take-off.

Once more down to the beach, dear friend.
Argh, the door's iced over again.
Just needs a bit of a KICK . . . stubborn thing . . . Ah, we're in.

Right, time for a swansong. Fingers crossed . . .

First time! That never happens. My lucky night after all.

OK then, here we go. Hold tight.

Carefully does it through the gears, a couple of notches and ready
on the handbrake. Keep it nice and steady . . .

I'm really opening her out now.

This may seem slow. But believe me, there's an optimum gritting
speed that mustn't be rushed. To do a thoroughly good job a job
must be done thoroughly.

I suppose I could talk you through the salt ratios that I've got in the
barrels, but life's too short. I will say, though, that it's good stuff.
Mined from the ancient sea-beds of Cheshire. It's all salt under Cheshire.
The Romans were at it. No doubt to grit the roads they were building.

The Victorians mined so much of it that the earth started sinking.
Houses would just disappear into the ground. Whole fields,
sucked under overnight.

In these blue-black hours, time disappears. It slips away completely
or freezes in the headlights.

I can feel it slipping.

These are the hours of the duty-bound, the lost souls and the enthusiasts.

You might think you see less working nights, but I disagree.
Out here I swear I see great white bears disappearing down cul-de-sacs
and narwhals trailing each other up and down the ditches. I've seen
angels in cherry trees and fallen stars on motorway roundabouts.

See how the full-beams light up the falling snow. All those tiny white flakes
so bright they could be stars ... or plankton. Nicer to think of it as gritting
through space rather than dredging the North Atlantic.

I'm a roving little night worm with two pale antennas,
chewing my way through the infinite blue.

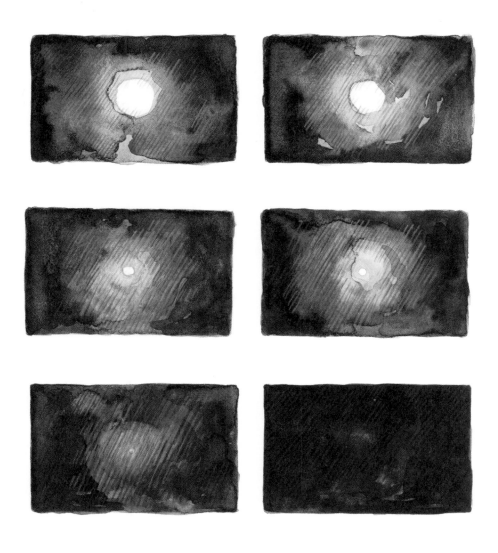

Argh this heater is total rubbish ...
There's the snooker hall and the post office.

I tell myself that I'll fix it for next year but I never do ...
There's the old pub, the police station and the tanning salon.

Suppose there's no point now ...
That's the vet and the supermarket car park.

Crumbly old things the pair of us.
The builders yard ... scrapyard ... graveyard.

Sometimes it feels like I'm the only person awake in the whole country. People might find that a lonely thought. Not me. Being alone and loneliness aren't the same thing.

I think of all those chilly feet sticking out the bottoms of duvets. The millions of pillow-squished faces. Snorers, nose whistlers, restless wrigglers and tightly tucked twitchy types. All those babies about to wake up and scream in their first Christmas morning.

It'll be dawn soon.

The whole world'll turn from blue to gold,
and then say what you like, it won't bring back the night.

Ooh, excuse me, I've got a bit of chow mein stuck in me molars.
The corner of a Christmas card doubles up nice as a toothpick.
That'll get it.

I can't go home now. Back to number 25 with nothing to
look forward to. A life without gritting's no life at all.

I decide when I've done my round.

Buses have stops and trams have rails. But I'm free.
I can go where I please.

So I will carry on. Through elevenses and well past lunch.
Beyond the A-roads and the B-roads.

Beyond the country lanes and the dirt tracks and further afield than
the furthest field, and if the van holds, grit beyond the sunset.

Outside any council jurisdiction. Outside gravitational jurisdiction.

Into the sky.

Into the clouds to grit . . . at . . . source.

Further and further. To where the stars, like cats' eyes, mark my route.

Until the grit's all gone and I switch off the barrels.

Turn off the slide-door freezer, the Mobile Sales
Chimer and the illuminated fibreglass 99s.

Turn off the overhead reading light.

Turn off the hazard light.

Turn off the dimmers and then . . .

. . . the engine.

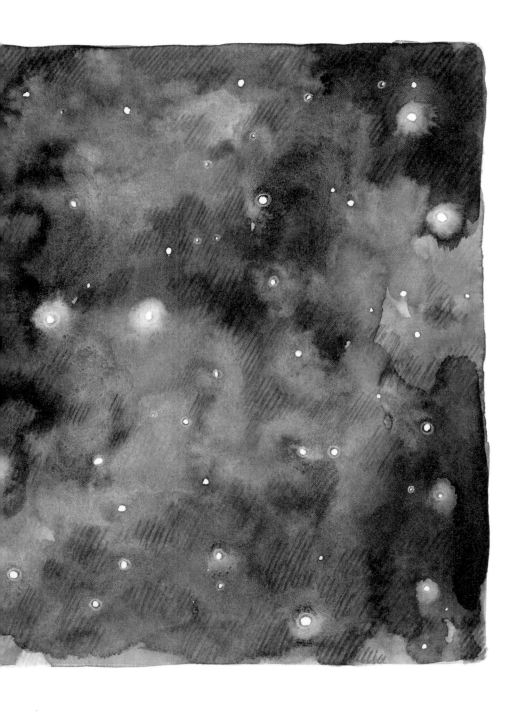

The End

With special thanks to Helen Conford, Annabel Merullo, John Reid, Markus
Dravs, Hugo Turquet, Marc Picken, Richard Bray, Laura McNeill,
Iain Berryman, Morad Khokar, Emma Bal, Ingrid Matts, Shoaib Rokadiya,
Katie Jarvis, Rebecca Lee and Richard Green.

Orlando Weeks studied illustration at Brighton University before spending a decade in the band, The Maccabees. In 2016, when the group decided to disband, he set about writing *The Gritterman*, his first book.